Five Ugly Monsters

by Tedd Arnold

SCHOLASTIC INC.

Cartwheel
B·O·O·K·S®

New York Toronto London Auckland Sydney

To Sean, Justin, Tera, Aaron, Kim, Mike T., Emilee, Laura, Crystal, Nicky,
Evan, Erin, Taylor, Joe, Mike J., Benjamin, Krystle, Lindsey, Diana,
Daniel, John, Terry, and Mrs. Callas, third grade, 1994

—T.A.

ISBN 0-590-22764-5

12   11   10   9   8   7   6   5   4   3   8   9/9   0   1   2   3/0

Printed in the U.S.A   08

First Scholastic paperback printing, September 1998

Five ugly monsters

jumping on the bed.

One fell off and
bumped its head.

Called for the doctor and the doctor said,

"No more monsters jumping on the bed!"

Four ugly monsters

jumping on the bed.
One fell off and
bumped its head.

Called for the doctor and the doctor said,

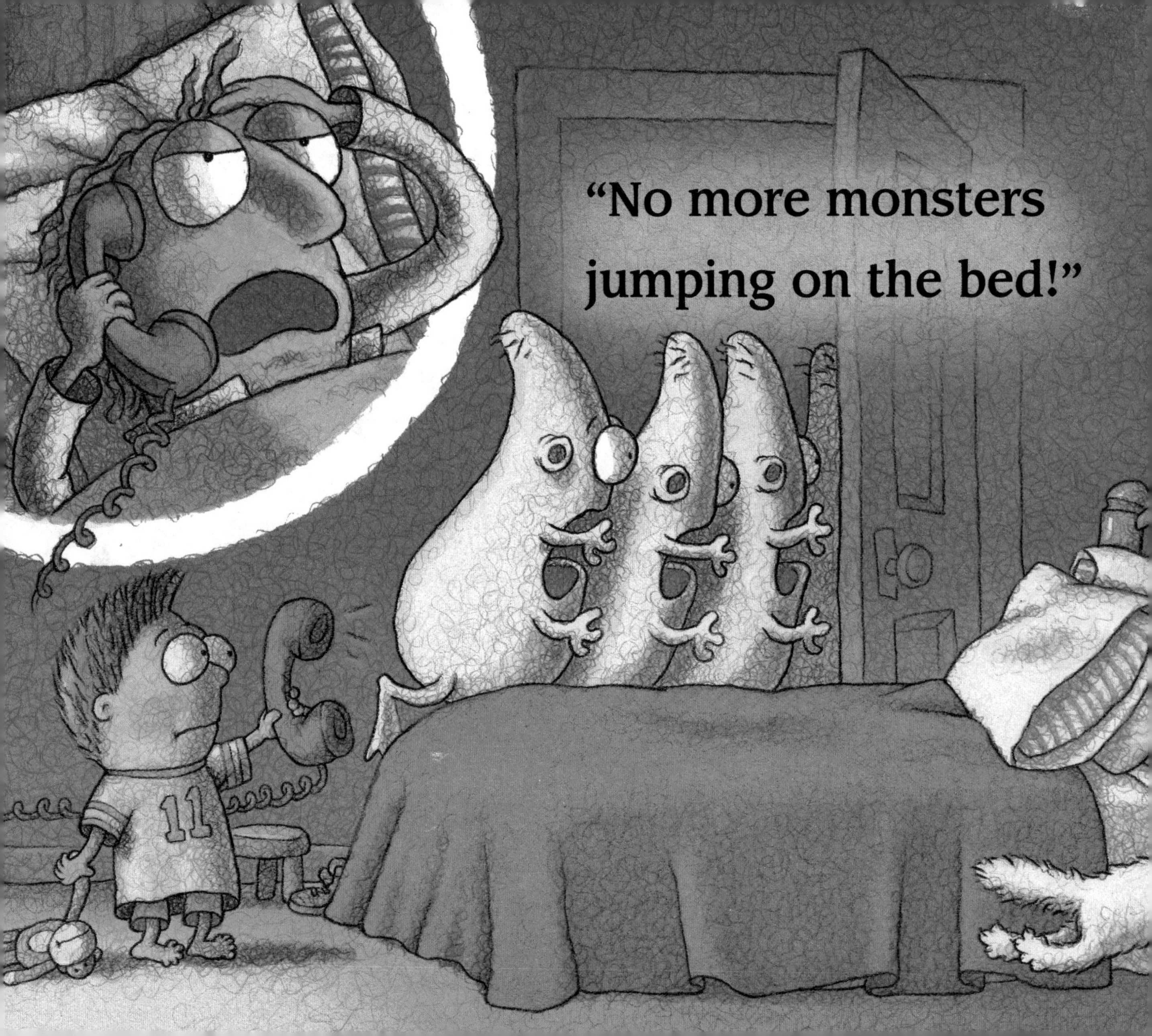

"No more monsters
jumping on the bed!"

Three ugly monsters

jumping on the bed.
One fell off and
bumped its head.

Called for the doctor and the doctor said,

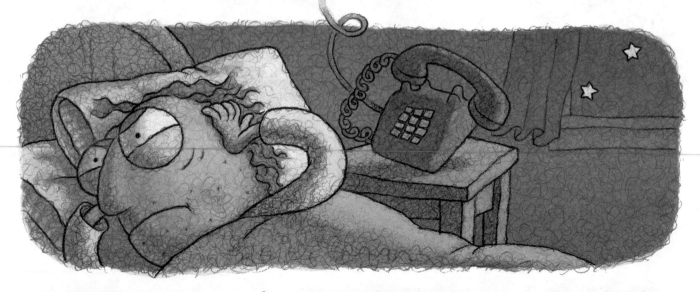

"No more monsters jumping on the bed!"

jumping on the bed.
One fell off and
bumped its head.

Called for the doctor and the doctor said,

"No more monsters jumping on the bed!"

One ugly monster

jumping on the bed.
It fell off and
bumped its head.

Called for the doctor and ...

"No more monsters

The end